Jeniffer Hess

DARKNESS AND THE BRIDE

bride in the darkness(an erotic, tenderness and

romance novel)

Copyright @ 2022 Jeniffer Hess
All right Reserve

This is a work of fiction Names Characters,Places and incident either are the product of the author's or imagination or are used fictitiously. Any resemblance of human being, business, companies, place of work is entirely coincidence.

Edited by Elizabeth Jason

Covered by Ruth Hovert

Thank you for picking me.

Catalog

About the book

In the warm mid-June afternoon, Julia's face was bright and shining with all of her beauty and uncontrollable joy. Her face was already red from the constant smiling. She was the bride, the event's focal point. Since her childhood fantasies, she had never experienced beauty and splendor like this. She had never put on her new dress

The Main Story

Mrs Thelma Schumacher sewed them all together. It was a floor-length wedding dress with a tulle-covered jewel necklace. Her brown hair was undone, with a few locks down and messy waves. A star-shaped, sparkling hairpiece served as her crown.

Nevertheless, she considered herself to be her greatest accessory. Buzz Meadows, her new husband, held her close. In Williston Falls, a dashing young man in a black tuxedo worked as a farmer. He wasn't a farmer, but rather a silo salesman.

She silently repeated her new name, the name she had gladly taken from him, throughout the ceremony and reception. Her brand-new moniker flowed effortlessly.

Attended by family and close friends in the Louise Hollis Community Center, the wedding was intimate and earthy, just like her life. Finger foods like Mrs. Schumacher's egg salad half-sandwiches, Mrs. Leann Schatz's lemon-drop cookies, and Mrs. Ruth Lathe's pink cupcakes were served at the small reception. Julia took a look at them from her seat at the desk. She enjoyed the realization that she was now a married woman like them, as she had hoped and waited, as they sat at the fold-out tables with their husbands. Merely without the knowledge or angst that each of them experienced with their husbands. Mr. Schatz had once advised her to take advantage of the fleeting moments when she had nothing to be unhappy about because the reasons would soon become clear. Mrs. Schatz had grunted and turned away upon hearing that, murmuring, "Took me about ten minutes." See?" As she ran off, Mr. Schatz had said. Julia didn't pay attention to their arguments about their hardened marriage.

She finally got the start of her life she had always wanted on her wedding day. She was about to embark on a brand-new life as a wife, mother, and woman. Because she lacked a gold wedding band on her fourth finger on her left hand, she was not a little girl to be swished away. She gained significance thanks to that new band. It gave her a voice among the Williston Falls women.

Julia threw her white peony bouquet over her head at the end of the wedding reception as she was about to leave with her husband. Jane, her ten-year-old younger sister, caught it. Mrs. Margaret Busch, their mother, snatched the bouquet from Jane's hands and sternly warned her, albeit politely, that she would not be married for many, many years and should dispel any notion of such a thing in order to ward off her growing desire to wear a white dress and consider immature boys to be suitable suitors.

As they raced from the community center to the idling, fire engine red 1959 Cadillac Coupe de Ville, Julia and Buzz were lavished with rice. Julia outright vetoed the idea, deciding that she would be laughed at for the rest of her life and that the wedding would be remembered solely for the tractor, not Julia. Buzz had wanted to chug away on a grain harvester straight from Mr. Hamilton's field. She stated to Buzz, "It would ruin my day." She simply touched his blond hair, despite his objection. Not only that, but she had displayed the womanly traits that she had always had.

Julia looked out of the community center and saw the shadows getting longer and the setting sun.

Like a valet, Mr. Achenbach opened the car door for them. He sold them the car at a low rent price because he was the only car dealer in Williston Falls. She wished she could get the car for free on this day. It could be regarded as a present. Instead, the Achenbachs provided candleholders. After circling the vehicle, Buzz slid in behind the hefty steering wheel. Sitting on the long bench seat, Julia smiled as she waved through the passenger window at the cheering, hooting, and chanting crowd. Julia noticed Mrs. Latte among the many exuberant expressions. She was looking in a different direction, and she had the same smug grin and dark eyes she had on the day she told the women about the Silhouette. When Mrs. Latte turned back toward the bride, Julia stopped waving in the middle of the motion. A large shadow was looming. The great oak tree was there, but in its upper branches was something darker. Mrs. Latte was aware. Julia was aware of its presence. Julia began to wave once more as she came to. Excited and overjoyed for the newlyweds, the faces were bright and shining.

The bumper-attached tin cans clanked and bonked as Buzz sped away from the curb.

We're hitched, Julia! We are finally married! In his excitement, Buzz yelled and hit the steering wheel with his hand.

It's so wonderful to contemplate. We've been waiting so long," she stated".

"I want to send you packing right now." Buzz pulled Julia down the bench scat close to him and wrapped his arm around her neck. He gave her a forehead kiss. Feeling the sun-warmed black tuxedo and Stetson cologne's woodsy, rugged scent, she rested her head on his shoulder.

Are you prepared for me? Are you ready for some fun, wifey? Buzz inquired.

Julia replied, "Of course." She was thrilled that Buzz, the man she loved, would finally be there. She would be able to satisfy him and give herself completely to him, allowing him to act as he pleased for both her and his benefit. In addition, she had waited for this chance to please. She could now simply say, "Take me." They had been apart throughout their relationship.

Buzz parked the car outside of town at the Harrow House, a small motel.

Simply enter the room. Buzz stated, "I will get us checked in and then bring in our suitcases." He gave his new wife a kiss and gave her a single key to the door with a pink ribbon on it.

She gave Buzz a glance. His dark tuxedo and neatly trimmed hair made him look attractive. Because he was hers, she kept her eyes on him. When the lobby door finally closed, she turned away.

Room No. was unlocked by Julia.23. With a single bed in the middle and an armchair by the window, the room was small. A card was next to a bottle of sparkling grape juice on the nightstand.

She felt awkward as she moved toward the card and the bottle. After her, the door shut behind her.

Honey? "Buzz?" She inquired.

No response was given. The space became unsettling. It got darker.

"Buzz?" She spoke softly, "Please don't make fun of me.

She returned to look through the thick, gloomy curtain. Nobody was present. She yanked it completely open for tranquility and to dispel any fears.

After that, Julia heard the bathroom faucet begin to drip water. Buzz was at the front desk, so she knew he couldn't be here.

"Jared?" She stated, "You are not welcome here. This is my and Buzz's time alone.

Because Buzz's best man enjoyed pulling pranks, it might not have been his idea to stage a gag.

Still apprehensive, Julia walked cautiously to the bathroom door, expecting Jared to run out and frighten her. She glanced around the corner, but no one was there.

The faucet is only fully open.

"Hello? Who is "there?" Angry, her voice cracked.

She stopped when she stepped onto the cold linoleum flooring in the bathroom.a long, gloomy shadow that was not caused by blocked light, but by a darker form. It started at the tips of her toes and went along the floor, over the bathtub's side, up the tiled wall, and onto the ceiling.

She covered her mouth after exhaling. You are present.

After the night Leann introduced them, she had been with him twice more. Those nights of hunger had been fascinating. She was left irrational, ravaged, with excessive salivation and breathing. The most pressing need was for more.

Julia touched the wall with her forward reach."Hello," she said in a cool, deep voice. She ran her hand along the tile. The length was then touched by her. The cock she desired was immediately in her grip on the Silhouette's warm, dark cock. She then considered her husband and the dick, his dick, whom she had anticipated loving. She was curious about how different they would be. Not only that, but she would receive a brand-new love experience whenever Buzz entered the room. The cock in her hand then snapped. She examined it. From head to toe, she felt a burning desire. She nevertheless decided that one kiss on the Silhouette would suffice, knowing that her husband would appear briefly. That would be all there is. She knelt forward and placed one knee on the tub's edge. She thought back to the most recent time the Silhouette had visited her, pressing her lips against the stark darkness.

Not only that, but she had stayed with her sister and her family while they sorted out any last-minute problems and arranged the wedding's final details.

In the country, Margaret and her family lived in a lovely two-story house. It was situated on a hill close to a covered, red bridge that crossed a raging stream.

Margaret dashed out of her farmhouse's front door as soon as she saw Julia get out of the taxi, and Julia dropped her suitcase at her feet. Hugs were exchanged between the sisters as they squealed. They had been together for a whole year. Margaret got married, moved, and soon had a child in the last 15 years. She was busy, focused on her family and home, and away from Julia during those three significant events in her life.

I am ecstatic that you are here. We have a lot to do," Margaret told Julia while reembracing her as if to verify her authenticity.

The couple began planning their wedding early the following day. Gray storm clouds made the sky look darker throughout the morning. The creek water that was flowing beneath the covered bridge had been raised by afternoon rain showers. Late that evening, a torrential downpour pounded the windows and roof.

Margaret's husband Harold had gone to bed, and her two young sons were also asleep as they worked. Finally, during the early hours of the morning, Margaret informed Julia that she was worn out and that Harold and her sons would wake her up shortly to begin her day. Julia then made her way to the guest room. It was directly above Margaret and Harold's bedroom on the second floor.

Coco, the family's dark tabby cat, came with her upstairs because Julia was staying in the cat's room, as Margaret had stated. The quaintness of the room pleased her. A slender bed, a dark oak armoire, a floor lamp with a dome shade that cast a soft orange light onto the ceiling and around the room, a wooden wicker rocking chair, and a bed.

As the raindrops hit the window, Julia sat back in the rocker and moved slowly. Coco jumped into Julia's lap and cradled herself well there. She gave the cat a gentle rub. Julia appreciated being away from the Schatz family. The couple had grown weary of her presence as well. The Schatz family's home was too small for three. Leann had also become distant and belligerent following the Silhouette's visit that stormy night. She would frequently glare across the living room at Julia. At Margaret's, Julia could now be herself. Even her nephews were happy to have her here.

Buzz and the wedding day entered Julia's dreams. The elaborate invites. The dress she had envisioned. The flower arrangement. She longed for the day when everyone would be watching her as she walked down the aisle. Most importantly, her husband Buzz Meadows's gaze. At the thought of becoming Mrs. Buzz Meadows soon, she could not stop smiling.

Coco's claws emerged as soon as her ear perked up. Despite the sharp grip, Julia was unable to see or hear anything. Coco's claws poked through Julia's nightgown and scratched her thighs, while the fur on her back stood. "Ow! Coco, take it easy. Nothing is amiss." She spoke to her like a mother and coddled her like a baby. You're too empathetic. Everything runs smoothly. I'm present.

Coco let go. She settled back into Julia's arms. The hallway then shook violently. Coco and Julia both heard it. Coco gave a soft purr this time. Once more, the rattle sounded. Coco took a small leap from Julia's lap and ran toward the door. The noise became a stampede and grew in volume until the guest room door was quickly knocked on.

Margaret dashed inside without waiting for Julia. Her face was pale with worry, and she was breathing heavily.

"How are you doing?" She stutters.

I'm okay. Did you believe there was a problem? Julia inquired.

"A loud ka-bang occurred. Then, my bedroom's overhead light started to wobble as if it were about to fall. I reasoned that you must have fallen or thrown something extremely heavy. I felt sorry for you.

Julia surveyed the area. Here, nothing got lost. I'm certain I didn't fall. What about the young men?

"Downstairs, their room is next to ours. This floor produced the sound. Additionally, "I peeked in their room before I came," she added.

"The other room up here can be checked." Julia got up. Margaret was in charge.

Margaret reassured herself, "I know I heard something fall." Even Harold heard it, but he didn't worry about it. I was told to ignore it. Typical of a man.

Julia's room was vacated by the two sisters. They arrived at the other bedroom on the second floor after carefully walking down the short hallway. Margaret started the process. She switched on the light. The sewing room was located inside. It was messy in the room. On multiple tables, rolls of fabric in various designs and colors.

Before sneaking in, Margaret looked around the room. She walked by the three torso mannequins draped in unfinished blouses, as well as the two sewing machines.
Julia was surprised when she looked in.

"The room is full! You're growing up to be like Grandma.

Julia guffawed.

As Julia disrupted her stealthy entrance to the room, Margaret's arched back and tensed shoulders eased.

Margaret continued her search for what might have fallen, saying, "It's a hobby with benefits—for me, my sons, and Harold." She quickly took long strides out of the room to avoid the supplies.

"Find something?" Julia inquired.

She answered, "No." She was still perplexed by everything. Something had to have been there. The thud was so loud it could have been nothing. She patted her chest as her tense shoulders eased even more. I surrender. I have no idea. This is so perplexing.

"Perhaps the storm."

The house will then have a hole in it. Perhaps the roof. Margaret shut the door and turned off the light. And you say you haven't heard anything?"

"Coco did, but I didn't. She either heard it or knew something about it. I was even scratched by her.

If Harold hadn't heard it, "I would say it was a dream."

She was reassured by Julia. Lay down and return to your bed. Take some time off because you need to get up soon.

"If I may. "Margaret ran her hand along the banister as she descended the stairs. Yes, if possible.

"Please know that I'm fine. And as far as we can tell, nothing has fallen here. Thus, there is no issue. Julia grinned at her rambunctious sister. Margaret divorced Julia.

She considered rocking back and forth in the chair when she was alone once more, but it seemed unlikely that that would have been the sound that woke Margaret. It was too muffled.

Coco walked between Julia's feet and rubbed her. Are you looking for more attention? She sat on the bed's edge and picked up the cat. From her back to the tip of her tail, she stroked. How is that, child? Yes, you like it, huh?

Coco purred as she meowed.

When Julia heard footsteps thudding up the stairs and a rumbling downstairs, she was enjoying the peace and quiet. Margaret barged in rather than knocking.

She stated, "You're going to upset Harold and wake the boys if you don't stop causing a racket."

Coco jumped to the floor from Julia.

"Me?"

"Yes, you do! Margaret continued to hold the bedroom door in her hand. Who else is atop this?

"It's just me, and all I'm doing is petting Coco here or wherever she went. In case the rocking chair were making any noise, I also stayed out of it.

Julia, seriously, don't. When Harold is angry, it's hard to control him.

"I will sleep on the couch." She fell onto the bed, arms outstretched, and her hair exploded behind her head as she did so. She rolled over and looked at her older sister while resting her head on her hand.

Look at that! Margaret growled, recalling the times Julia had irritated her as a child. You were doing it, and I knew it. Avoid teasing. Simply fall asleep. Tomorrow, we'll work on the wedding. Even lunch for you will be included.

"Aw! Sounds fun, said Julia.

With her eyes wide, Margaret warned, "We won't go" if she heard anything else.

I won't say anything because it wasn't me! Stay away from this area if you hear anything more. Margaret caught Julia's gaze.

Margaret let go of the door's tight grip. Be nice.

Julia said, "You sound just like Mom did" as she shut the door. Threats in general."

"Shut up!" Julia heard through the door.

When Julia sensed the impending outburst of laughter, she hid her giggling as best she could by shoving her face into the pillow alone in the room. She hadn't received a motherly reprimand like that in a long time. She felt like a young child. Likewise, she and Margaret used to squeal with uncontrollable laughter when their parents were angry with either Margaret or her. As a result, Margaret and she would escape to the bedroom and laugh into their pillows.

When Coco sat down next to Julia on her chest and quietly begged for attention, Julia's urge to giggle lessened. She soon stopped laughing as she stroked the cat.

Julia climbed out of bed to dim the lights before she got too tired. Only Coco's darting eyes could be seen in the pitch-black. Julia sat down next to the cat after taking off her nightgown. Coco ran off with a brief yip.

What did you do? I apologized. I didn't mean to lay on you. In the dark, she patted the bed. After that, she yipped when she felt what she initially thought was Coco with her hand. She brushed the cat's now-slim, warm body with her hand once more. Contrary to Coco's thick coat, it lacked fur. And when she touched it, it pulsated.

"Coco?" She grumbled.

When the cat brushed against Julia's nose and cheek, Julia withdrew her hand from the hairless body. She jumped out of bed and brushed her hand off as if it were smeared with filth when she realized that Coco was at her face and that her hand was on something else. Julia returned to the chair after putting Coco back on the bed. Her skin crawled up her back and her body was jittery.

"What did that mean?" She inquired.

She could only picture a body covered in blood. Absurd, but the thought scared her enough to make her leave the room and run downstairs right away. She rang the doorbell in Margaret's bedroom.

"Maria, Maria!" She maintained a controlled hiss in her voice.

With rage covering her face, Margaret opened the door. What's next?

I'm afraid. Upstairs, the bed has something in it.

Margaret positioned her hips with her hands. I'm really getting annoyed by you. I'd rather sleep. Not only that, but I'm getting sick of your games.

This is not a contest. I'm extremely terrified. She put her head on her sister's chest and wrapped her arms around her. The bed has something there. Do your children engage in such pranks?"

"As in, what? Upstairs, they don't keep dead bodies. You and I have already looked up there. You stated that nothing existed. What then might it be?

"I'm not sure. I don't want to learn. Can I sleep here, maybe on the couch? Julia inquired.

"I guess, but Harold and I will be up soon," she replied.

That is acceptable. I will return upstairs when there is light.

Fearful of the night. Ha! Well, a blanket is there. Margaret indicated a folded crocheted blanket on the couch's arm.

"The one that my mom crocheted. I'm grateful. Julia gave up her worry and gave her sister a bigger hug. She sat down on the sofa.

"You are truly afraid. I nearly lost my breath because of you.

"I know. "She cuddled up in the orange-and-brown-striped blanket as she pulled it over her.

Margaret wished Jules "sweet dreams."

"Mm hmm. "As Julia settled in, she mumbled a nonsense response. Her lips were set in a smooching smile, and she had her eyes closed.

Margaret returned to her bed and glanced over her shoulder once more at her terrified younger sister, who was about to become a man's wife. Jules, you need to grow up. Fast-growing up.

At that precise instant, there was an abrupt thunderous boom that appeared to be low and directly overhead. As a response, Margaret shut down and hid her head. Julia remained silent.

Margaret shook Margaret's shoulder when Julia awoke later. Harold was approaching the kitchen. If you want to sleep in, go upstairs.

After a mute nod, Julia walked up the staircase like a zombie. She settled down on the guest room bed. She was settling in when she felt a warmth along her back come up against her.

Not only that, but she mumbled groggily, "Morning, Coco."

Coco was sitting in the rocking chair across the room when she opened her eyes. However, the warmth on her back persisted for her.

She felt nothing when she patted the bed behind her. Not even the strange sensation she experienced last night. Only the mattress and blanket remained. Her mind became drowsy, and she fell back asleep.

A storm was pounding, and the day was dark when Julia awoke. The rainwater had made new streams emerge from the drain spouts, forcing the stream to rise even higher than the day before.

Not in a long time has it rained like this. It won't please the farmers, I know. The fields don't like too much rain. Can wreak havoc on crops," Harold declared while standing in front of a large window. The glass was being soaked by rivers of rain.

Can we venture outside? Margaret's son inquired.

Yes, we are drained. "Let's go into the creek," said her other son.

Margaret turned to face them. You can't do that!

Julia began to participate in the boys' begs. Yes, we're bored, Margie. When do you intend to take us somewhere?"

Margaret said with a dry, angry look reminiscent of a mother, "Julia."

Harold stepped in. Send them someplace.

"Have you got some cash? "Margaret shot back.

"Just get rid of them. "His hand was flapping in the air. It will benefit everyone."

"Is it going to help me? Margaret stated, "I'm the chauffeur. "She quietly ran around the house in anger. She quickly gathered the boys and her sister and set out for town with them.

They came back exhausted but upbeat hours later. Margaret and Julia organized the ceremony and assigned various roles to ensure that the day ran smoothly as they worked on the wedding. Margaret was worn out as the sky finally got dark.

I'm off to sleep. Do you believe you will be able to sleep upstairs tonight? Don't do it, if you can't. Tonight, I don't want to be bothered.

Julia replied, "You have become the ideal mother. " Straightforward and direct.

I must maintain order in this location. You'll see what unsupervised children can do to a house.

Julia let out a sigh of anticipation. I hope I won't have to put kids in groups. A full house of them! Small Meadows."

Margaret gave her a mocking stare. Now you say that. Before you have a second child, I'll ask again. Cowboys and mothers go horseback riding. Mothers also have a harder job. Cowboys cannot converse with cows.

Julia guffawed.

Julia said, "I'll sleep upstairs. "I won't do anything to wake you up, like jump around. I'm also worn out.

Julia climbed onto the bed as she entered the guest room. She recalled doing numerous things as a child to irritate her sister. She silently chided herself while lying still.

Not only that, but she got dressed in her nightgown and sat down in the middle of the bed. Likewise, she listened to the rain fall through the window while lying on her back.a steady beat with irregular beats that calmed her. Her eyes began to bulge. To keep them open was hard. She sat back and let her arms spread out, hanging over the bed's edges. Over the end of the bed, her feet dangled. Her bare feet started to get very warm. At her ankles, she could feel her pulse. Thinking she needed to increase blood flow, she wiggled her legs and scrunched her toes until her feet started to itch. Her foot struck a person as she jerked.

She got up and moved to the bed's edge. I'm so sorry, Coco! Where are you now? Cat, allow me to hold you. I'm so sorry.

She looked over the bed, but Coco was not there. She then experienced a larger presence. It loomed large and high above her. Dark and sexual, it was. Julia felt a consuming heat that spread from her feet to the rest of her body, despite the fear it evoked in her.

"Is that you?" She spoke softly.

Julia noticed a presence, but there was no audible response. The Silhouette had an incredible aura. The Silhouette was only visible to her eyes as an unsubstantiated haze, similar to a sheer curtain hanging far away from a window. However, the rest of her knew for sure.

She felt like a little girl in a candy store when she saw it. She wanted to touch the Silhouette and have a good time. Her deep urge was neither pushy nor aggressive. Instead, that childish absurdity surged within. The mattress's springs chirped as her feet tapped the floor and her butt bobbed happily on the bed. As a deterrent to all of these urges, she placed her hands between her knees.

She felt joy return in the darkness. There was a lively sense of anticipation for what might, might happen, and would happen.

She received sufficient responses to all of these surges and joy.

Julia whispered, "You've been away from me." I've been missing you.

As a means of welcoming a lover she had desired, she reached out to the hazy figure in front of her. When she touched it, she also jumped. Hard, long, and terrifyingly big. She realized that the sensation that so terrificd her last night was exactly this.

Shc remembered that the length had been more prominent in the past when she had been with the Silhouette. Because it had been a heady internship that culminated in a single night of fear, lust, and Mrs. Schatz, the first time couldn't count. Julia was able to fully enjoy the Silhouette's pleasures and power in the subsequent encounters.

She was pushed back onto the bed when the Silhouette stepped forward over her. Its essence slid through her open legs, through her buttocks, under her nightgown, between the fabric and Julia's flesh, over her bare shoulders, and around her long neck, softly covering her. It was like lying on the beach and letting the waves crash over her head and hair, from her toes.

She eased her breathing by slowly raising her chest and then gently moaning as her chest fell. Julia's face became brighter as a result of the Silhouette's goodness. She felt reenergized.

She told the ghost, "Don't wait," and then waited for a while. Not only that, but she begged, "Please, because I have denied myself for months," feeling nothing more.

In order to direct the Silhouette toward her supple, wet pussy, she felt between her legs.

"Do you like to know that I held back pleasure for you?" She inquired.

The massive dick was too far between her legs for her to feel. She sat up, confused and already heated. She was pinned to the mattress and pushed flat by a pressure on her chest. Her chest was covered in a thick layer of gloomy mist. The Shapeless, Its dark cock also got in her fresh mouth. She naturally tightened her lips. However, the pressure became too much, and she continued to resist, acting like a child rejecting a bad medicine.

She waved her hands through the hanging mist until she finally wrapped them around a darkness she could see. As a result, the massive mass pressed even harder on her mouth. While turning her head to one side and the other, she tried to pull it away from her. She fought and exhaled through her nose, making the sound of an irate animal. No! I'm not prepared.

The Silhouette wanted to be in her mouth, she was aware of. However, she had never previously permitted such a filthy "thing" to enter her mouth. I thought of Mrs. Schumacher. Her account of waking up that morning with a salty taste in her mouth and dried gunk on her face. Instead, Julia desired the Silhouette of her pussy, where she had always loved it and where it had always gone. Strange was this unexpected experience. It was inappropriate. She hated thinking of the phrases that would describe what she would do:Dick sucking." She was offended by the phrase by itself. Not only that, but she rubbed her eyes.

She turned and fought the Silhouette and its demanding demands. The Silhouette, on the other hand, possessed tremendous tenacity and strength. The woman who was thrilled to see her secret lover and the giddy young girl were both gone. She had struggled alone to avoid becoming "one of those women, if they actually could be called 'women,'" as Mrs. Schatz had put it.

She loosened her lips at thc mere thought of speaking, and wanted to bet the Silhouette once more that it would let her be. The Silhouette made use of this.

She took the length into her mouth. It filled her, causing her to feel anxious and tense in her body.

AHer confusion was caused by a feeling of being confined. Too big was the cock. It pressed into her cheek, pressed into the back of her throat, and rubbed against the top of her mouth, over her tongue. She choked. Then it slightly retracted. Her struggle went away. The terror briefly subsided. The Silhouette then slowly moved forward and back as it entered her mouth gently and more deeply. Fears dissipated as it became more gentle. Strangely, she discovered that it lacked sweetness and reminded her of the large lollipops she used to love as a child. Each week, she had spent her allowance on these popsicles. Grape, strawberry, and even the sour-sweet flavor of black licorice.

She allowed her tongue to touch and examine the cock. She began sucking quickly. After circling the great cock's crown with the tip of her tongue, she let the dick's underside rub her tongue. The cock briefly jerked as a result. It continued to rock. To keep up with the beat, she bobbed her head off the pillow. She relaxed as she let go of the blanket with her hands and looked at what she couldn't exactly see. Her hands wobbled in opposition to the thrusts, finding the Silhouette's shaft and then the low-hanging balls. As soon as she held them in her hands, she felt a second jolt. The rocking got worse and faster. After that, a lot of warmth flew out of her mouth, swelling her cheeks. Juice that was thick. She swallowed a lot of it, but there was so much that it drained out of her mouth.

Except for the cum, she realized her mouth was empty. The cock had vanished. She didn't have any weight on her chest. The feeling of being enclosed was gone.

She wiped her mouth on the blanket and spit out the cum.

Are you still around? She questioned quietly:Don't leave me so quickly. I require more of you.

However, there was no response or presence in the room.

She jumped onto her lap with only Coco.

"Return soon. I only have a short amount of time before...

She stated, "I wasn't talking to you, kitty."

Julia was sad, depressed, and alone when she pet Coco's back. She considered Buzz.

She gave the big dick a kiss while leaning on the edge of the bathtub in her white wedding dress. It was as she had remembered it. She put it in her mouth after her one kiss turned into multiple kisses. The girth and warmth were excellent. She inhaled as much as she could. She let out a little saliva from the corners of her mouth after the Silhouette gave her a push.

The door to the motel room suddenly opened.

"Julia!" Buzz called out her name with glee. Are you uncovered?

Despite some resistance, she retreated.

She whispered, "I'll see you soon, but not today."

Buzz once more called, "Julia."

"Here, my brand-new husband." She came out smiling.

She wrapped her arms around him as he rushed toward her.

Buzz stated, "I've waited so, so long for this." Let's get busy now!

He shimmied across the room, funnily. He would have wrecked the mood if it weren't for love.

Not only that, but he said, "You must be thrilled as well."a little something in her mouth from the corner of her mouth."

She was embarrassed and wiped it off. It was due to her other partner.

"My love, I've been getting ready for you. My solitary love.

The curtain at the window swung as a dark shadow moved across the room.

In their new life together as husband and wife, Buzz and Julia fell to the hard mattress.

Conclusion

I'd like to express my gratitude once more for downloading this book.

I hope you are aware of the significance and necessity of a couple participating in and fully participating in their sexual experiences by this point. Everything is done in a hurry, in a hurry, in today's world. Whatever it is about our relationships, conversations, food, or sex, everything is being done quickly. Since quickies and casual sex are now the norm, no one has time to have a sexual experience that goes beyond physical boundaries. There is so much more to lovemaking than just having sex;it entails developing a relationship with your partner. You will need to be conscious at first to make sure you are following the steps in this book, but eventually, all of this will come naturally to you. You will need to put in a lot of time and effort into this process if you want to see some good results. Keep trying and don't give up because mastering these strategies will take some time.

Thank you, and best wishes.